The Length
of Now

The Length of Now

Stories | Poems | Photos

DAVID RALPH JOHNSON

THE LENGTH OF NOW
Copyright © 2021 David Ralph Johnson
All Rights Reserved.
ISBN: 9780578933993

DEDICATION

To Casey and Maddie.

Thank you.

Table of Contents

Phrases on a Page

To write, I cast a net

Over my memories

And pull hard.

The good and the bad

Come sagging up

Dripping and intertwined.

Do I really want to relive the pain

In exchange for phrases on a page?

Change the names

To protect the innocent?

Who protects me?

I place that last question aside,

Embrace the pain, and

Let ambition crack the whip.

STORIES

Old Man Down

St. Paul Lowertown, Minnesota

2018

The dome of the Minnesota State Capitol reflected briefly in the bank of windows on the north wall of the State History Museum as I darted by. The buildings sat opposite each other a quarter mile apart, with a concrete canyon carrying I-94 traffic between them. The dome's white marble curves followed the arch of the museum's windows in perfect harmony. I would recall that later, but just then had no time to ponder anything but my hair-raising descent on two wheels down the 12th Street sidewalk and over the freeway.

Destination Lowertown.

I'd taken training earlier in the day on the Capitol mall to learn how to safely ride an e-Scooter. Two young Public Safety Department staffers, fit and tech-savvy, provided instruction to me and a small group of my Transportation Department coworkers. The e-whiz kids began by showing how to start an e-Scooter with a mobile phone. Sound advice followed. "Wear a suitable helmet. Test the brakes before you get rolling. Top speed of fifteen miles an hour isn't the time to realize you're missing either one." After some questions and answers, they got on, hit the throttles, and circled us in convincing smooth steady lines.

Now it was our turn. A few daring souls gave the e-Scooters a try. I watched as they did very well, looping the mall plaza like a kettle of land hawks gliding the capitol terrain with ease.

On foot to my Lowertown apartment after work, I came up to a freestanding e-Scooter. By chance, a kid zipped past riding one of the same. He was crouched to break the wind, milking as much speed out of the skinny rig as possible. Inspired, my eighteen-year-old brain kicked in and jumped my sixty-six-year-old body onto the e-Scooter platform next to me. Startup engaged; I was gone.

What an amazing ride. After mastering the steep 12th Street descent, I flew the city streets unfettered on electronic power sent from web-enabled heaven. The Jackson Street bikeway was reached in two minutes. South on its two open lanes took me straight to 5th Street, then a hard left pointed me home.

The expression on my face and those of the bystanders I passed melded into white toothy blurs.

My pedestrian days were over. This had to be shared. I stopped a block from the apartment and rang my wife.

"Hello."

"Theresa, look out the window."

Pause.

"Why, Dave?"

"You'll see."

Pause.

I hung up, remounted my chariot of fire, and took off.

Theresa caught my approach from our apartment window two stories above Mears Park and gave me a tentative what-the-heck-now-Dave wave.

Wave returned, I slowed to a crawl and readied to park. In the process, my front tire buried itself in the wood chips of a sidewalk tree and sent me crashing to the cement.

Kids on a park bench yelled, "Hey, old man down."

I rolled and popped upright. Hearing their alert, I scanned the area to help the old man.

Realizing the person of their concern was me, I gave them a not-to-worry thumbs up.

One kid tossed a "Nice recovery" back at me. I felt somewhat less elderly with that.

Given no broken body parts, Theresa wasn't too upset when I got upstairs, saying, "I thought your fall was a joke. Glad you didn't kill yourself."

Old man down, not old man dead. So far, so good in Lowertown.

• • •

Time Tool

"QeeeEeeQ, return now please. Second request. We repeat, second request."

QeeeEeeQ was on Earth hovering close behind a cave lion that was trailing a Neanderthal man, readying for the kill. QeeeEeeQ was so absorbed in the stealthy movements of the blonde-furred creature that he missed the first request from Mothership, the spacecraft that had deposited him on Earth and now waited in nearby outer space for his return.

The lion was about to snap the neck of the unaware Neanderthal with a noiseless pounce and a chomp of steel-vise jaws. "Barbaric," thought QeeeEeeQ, but he could not intervene. Interfering with another world's circumstances was strictly

7

forbidden by his fellow beings and subject to the Mothership Century Shun, a hundred-year loneliness stint that QeeeEeeQ did not want to repeat. One such shun imposed on him a few voyages back was all he needed for the rest of his centuries-long life.

QeeeEeeQ and his five hundred nine other extraterrestrial mates were visiting Earth for the day, a nice side trip from their shot across Earth's galaxy forty thousand years ago. The group had been spread out over Eurasia. QeeeEeeQ landed in the modern time province of Piloña in Northern Spain, Neanderthal territory back then in the Paleolithic age.

All but QeeeEeeQ had returned to Mothership. The crew's mounting discontent from above rang his brain. They were of one mind, sharing individual experiences telepathically as a collective whole. To squelch their angst, he reluctantly evaporated from Earth's surface and materialized onboard Mothership in the blink of his middle eye. He was welcomed grandly, all concern forgotten, and Mothership hit warp speed for points beyond.

—

The departure caused an explosion of light that flattened the cave lion to the ground in fear. Nmm, the Neanderthal, was shaded by a towering cliff. He was left shocked but able to see while the blind lion fumbled for sight.

White hot brightness had temporarily overexposed everything in view, but no horrendous thunder followed. The vacuum of outer space kept that in check. This was new lightning to Nmm. God-like. He bolted for home to tell others. Sight restored and scent gone, the cave lion stretched out for a nap to rest up for nocturnal pursuits later on.

Halfway to his cave, Nmm's eye caught something odd. Sunlight was emanating from a slight depression in the dusty path. As he approached, he saw an object that held the sun and sky magically on its visible surface.

The object was cylindrical, grippable, like the shaft of Nmm's spear, but short, extending just beyond the length of a Neanderthal palm with a completely foreign surface in shape and gloss. Nothing on Earth was so uniform. Things of nature were all curvy or jagged, and things Neanderthals made, like a spear tip, were rough-hewn. Bowls carved by Nmm for his wife Omm were coarse until smoothed by her repeated handling, and then still misshapen. Neanderthal language had no word for the object's pure form, no word for perfect.

"What an afternoon. Omm won't believe this," Nmm thought as he bent to pick up the object. His wife loved his sundown recounts of the day's foraging and hunting. Tonight would be special. But, as Nmm gasped the object he felt warmth and darkness, and in the next instant he was with Omm in their cave.

The object was still in hand, but Nmm was sitting next to a smoldering cook fire in the middle of an end-of-meal staredown with Omm—that had occurred two suns ago. Toddler Opp was on Omm's left breast getting his fill. Their staredown was for what remained of the adult meal, a few bites of savory moss and mushrooms. An Omm specialty. Neanderthals were very gentle people among themselves and depended on the staredown to resolve all disagreements, or challenges such as who would get the last bite that evening.

Nmm was completely flummoxed. The minute before he'd been walking the open plain and the next thing he knew, he was experiencing an evening meal from the past with Omm and Opp.

Omm took Nmm's startled look as a flinch and she polished off the tasty morsels. She gave him a wily smile, then peeled Opp away from her chest, burped him, and left for a diaper change to deal with the lumpy load in the triangle of hide that covered Opp's bottom.

Everything was the same as two evenings ago, the only difference being Omm's victory in the staredown.

—

Far out in space, QeeeEeeQ became frantic as he turned in his travel gear from the Earth visit. His time tool was missing. The time tool was along to learn other lifeform's ways, such as how a lion overtook a Neanderthal. Once something was observed, one could invoke the tool telepathically and go back in time to view the activity again, as many times as necessary to fully understand it.

Mothership had thousands of time tools in stock, so QeeeEeeQ's loss was not a supply issue.

However, when left behind, a time tool's potential for radically changing another lifeform's history was serious excrement—a Mothership Century Shun event for sure if not corrected.

The correction involved telepathically disabling the lost time tool, nullifying its power for time travel. At worst, it then became a simple tool or object d'art for the finder.

Given Mothership's warp speed and distance from Earth, the telepathic single would require generation by the entire crew. QeeeEeeQ's telepathic range was only the width of an average galaxy, way short for what was needed. The crew's collective signal would have the power to reach Earth in fourteen Earth days, or fourteen suns in Neanderthal terms.

Once the mishap was realized by QeeeEeeQ, the entire crew knew the story immediately.

"Damn collective thinking," he lamented to himself. Well almost to himself. He sighed. "OK all, let's begin the procedure…"

—

After the repeat meal with Omm and Opp, Nmm relived the next two days as best as he could recall. He felt more an observer than a participant, although he went through all the motions as before to not alarm anyone. This time though he was in possession of the lost time tool. He kept it close to his chest, suspecting it had great purpose yet to be understood. Delivery by a god via silent lightning was proof enough for him.

He mastered the tool's power in short order. He found that if he held the tool and wondered about it, he was sent back in time two suns. If he kept the tool in his hide pouch and did not wonder about it, he stayed put.

While Nmm was incapable of conscious telepathy to operate the tool to its full extent, his wondering about it sent a mild telepathic-like signal that triggered the tool's default time travel, that being two suns back.

As well as having the default, the tool was engineered with two failsafes that prevented disaster for the novice time traveler. Failsafe One. When Nmm was in the two suns back period, the tool would not let him go back further in time, keeping the default the default and Nmm not too far away from when he'd left. Failsafe Two. He could not repeat the same trip back, preventing him from inadvertently looping forever in an already visited time period.

He made two accidental trips back in time before he got the hang of it. Although unplanned, he put the time to good use in both cases. In the first he corrected an insult he had made to Omm about her new hairstyle that he hadn't noticed. That proved helpful later under the snooze hides. In the second he took better aim at a sheep that he had overshot before and single handedly took it down. His standing in the Neanderthal band rose a notch with that.

Knowing after those experiences that he could willingly go back in time, he kept watch for any dilemma he could go back to and resolve for his family or the Neanderthal band.

It wouldn't be long.

—

Back on Mothership, QeeeEeeQ's quick action and leadership to disable the lost time tool was looked upon favorably by all. He would serve no shun time.

He felt relieved that his ordeal was coming to a close. He hoped secretly that the time tool, in benign form, might someday decorate a nook in the cave of a nice Neanderthal family. It was beautiful. His companions, not secretly of course, felt the same.

The signal to shut down the time tool had flown along nicely without any complicating stellar interruptions. It was a bit ahead of schedule and would arrive in a few Earth minutes.

—

"Nmm, you should get the fire started."

"Right, Omm." Dusk was coming and there was rumor among the Neanderthal band of a cave lion in the area. A night fire at the cave entrance would be a good precaution to ward it off.

Nmm had Opp on his shoulders and was tearing around the woods near the cave entrance, growling like a bear.

"Grrrr. Grrrrrrr. Bear's gonna getcha. Grrrrrr."

Nmm's antics and Opp's bouncing giggles filled Omm's heart with complete happiness. She hated to end their frolicking, but it was getting dark.

"Come on boys. Please."

Nmm reached over his head and flew Opp into his mother's arms. Opp squirmed for kid freedom, made it to the ground, and toddled around as his dad went to the stack of firewood.

A stone's throw away, camouflaged in the brush, lay the cave lion. Rumor no more. Naturally blended into its surroundings. Invisible to the naked eye. Breath silent. The lion recognized Nmm from the day of lightning but drooled instead over the thought of devouring the little one. An adult was a bit of work to take down. He wasn't in the mood. Plus, there were two of them. But the toddler? A simple grab and go would do it. A tasty snack before the night's prowl. He inched forward.

Opp circled closer. His sweet toddler scent wafted in the lion's nostrils and the kill was on.

Omm saw it all. The brush parting. The lion's burst forward. Opp being lifted and carried off by his diaper.

Omm's scream sent shivers through Nmm. He had never heard something so terrifying leave her throat, a terror and fear voiced from the graves of her ancestors.

Nmm understood the tragedy immediately. He saw the last of the lion disappearing down the trail and no Opp to be found.

Omm was on her knees sobbing. Ignoring her was gut wrenching, but Nmm's only choice was to go and go now. He grabbed his spear and took off down the trail.

He knew what was going to happen. The chase was pointless. By then, the lion had a distance Nmm could not make up, off in any direction. Opp would be crushed in the lion's jaws shortly, if not already.

He stopped in his tracks and stabbed the ground repeatedly with his spear, killing the lion in his mind with bone-piercing ferocity. All his energy spent, he collapsed in tears and lay wishing he was dead with his son.

Hours had passed by the time Nmm had the strength to rise and go back to the cave. The trail was visible by starlight. In the semi-darkness he rolled over and felt the hardness of the time tool on his ribs. He realized, by the gods, that he had the means to reverse Opp's death. The joy of adrenaline overtook his body at the thought of going back to the past and killing the lion before it took his little Opp. Yes, he could do it. He would do it.

Nmm knew he must first console Omm. Reassure her that he would right the situation, although exactly how would be impossible to explain. He hardly understood it himself. She was in shock when he got to the cave, speechless from the loss of Opp. He gathered her in his arms and covered them both in a large bear skin. She was weeping softly, but calm when he slipped out from the bear skin for the trip back two suns. He unsheathed the time tool and gave it a strong wonder.

—

Perhaps there was a god, or gods in Earth's Paleolithic time forty thousand years ago. Or fate. Hard to know from old bones or permafrost findings. But some energy put something in the path of QeeeEeeQ's signal to prevent disablement of the time tool. The signal was deflected at the very second Nmm needed the tool most. And the tool worked as Nmm wondered.

Given the two days back, he had plenty of time to steel himself for the different kill. At the cave lion's leap, Nmm's spear found home deep in the lion's heart, dropping it a safe distance from Opp.

—

Years that followed were happy ones. Nmm headed off numerous disasters for the Neanderthal band and eventually was made leader. Omm made fetching necklaces from cave lion teeth. And Opp grew tall.

• • •

DAVID RALPH JOHNSON

Heartbreak Money

St. Paul, Minnesota

1979

"Donna, your fraud perp got arrested today."

Donna turned from her computer screen. She was being addressed first thing that morning by Mr. Pierce, vice president of ONE Bank's Midwest audit division. Mr. Pierce's pinstripes filled the narrow opening of Donna's cubicle, defining the contours of his executive body.

Donna smiled but said nothing. Her introverted self needed a minute to rise to the call for a response. Mr. Pierce didn't wait. He had executive places to be.

"Your work in pinpointing the perpetrator's theft was very impressive. All bank money will be recovered. Good work."

"Thank you, Mr. Pierce."

"ONE Bank would like to thank you with a bonus. You'll see it on your next paycheck."

Donna rose and shook Mr. Pierce's hand. She was dwarfed by his tall frame and had to look up to catch him directly in the eye. He liked that, plus her firm handshake. She had steeled herself in the past for this type of encounter, knowing that good eye contact and a solid grip told a person like Mr. Pierce that she was serious about herself and her career.

"Wonderful, sir. Glad to help."

Mr. Pierce departed. Donna sat down and swiveled in her chair. She stopped on the third spin, happy. "Wow," she thought, "The engagement party tonight, too. Brian will be so happy with the news of the money." She and her fiancé Brian were hosting a small get together that Friday night at Frosts, their local hang out, to celebrate their recent engagement.

"Oh my gosh. Much to do," she thought, and back to work she went.

—

Donna met Brian two years ago. They both reached for green beans at the same time in the bank cafeteria line. Their hands brushed together.

"Oh, take them please," was Brian's response. Donna did so with a shy smile.

The next day their paths crossed in the skyway that joined the bank's two buildings.

Brian said, "Green bean lady?"

"Yes, that was me." Donna thought about fleeing from the gorgeous man in front of her, but they had both paused. She felt promise in his hesitation. Mutual attraction. Brian read her eyes and was taken there too, that happenstance dot in the universe where two lonely souls find one another.

Donna broke the silence, "They were tasty." Geez almighty, she thought to herself, the green beans were tasty?

Brian laughed. "Good to hear," he said, then seized the moment. "I'm Brian Hensen. I'm a senior programmer in IT." He held out a confident hand.

Donna returned the gesture, shook his hand, and said, "Donna Benson. Audit."

They chatted a bit about work, then Brian said, "Hey Donna Benson, let's talk more tomorrow at the cafeteria for lunch. See you there?"

Spontaneity struck Donna. "Sure, Brian Hensen. See you there."

As they parted, Donna said quietly, "Benson meets Hensen. How nice."

From then on, the Benson-Hensen pair bloomed. Junk shopping on 7th street. Fancy meals at Frosts. Brian was non-stop fun the minute he and Donna were away from their sixty-hour-a-week jobs. He spent money like there was no tomorrow. Donna found his extravagance a puzzle given his IT pay, but she did not want to rock the boat in fear of dampening Brian's spirit, or worse yet losing his love.

These concerns faded the night he proposed.

"Donna, I hope to share my life with you. Will you marry me?" He slipped an antique diamond ring on her finger; one she had admired recently when window shopping on 7th street. He never missed a thing.

"Of course, Brian. Of course." She beamed; her future now secured.

"Twenty-one. Dealer wins." That was it for Brian. Wednesday, near midnight, and all his cash was gone. Brian left the card game with eyes down. He was $75,300 in debt, an insurmountable figure given his salary. His gambling addiction was a dark secret, and the last two years romancing Donna made for a death spiral of debt, the finale being her ring costing $8,000. He could no longer juggle all the payments.

The solution came to Brian at work the next day. He was testing the bank's dormant account report. He had written program code to resolve a minor report glitch. The report listed customer accounts with no transactions in the last five years. It was used by bank staff to send dormant account money to the state treasury once the five-year limit was reached. Some account balances were in the thousands.

"How could someone with that much money ignore it for five years?" he wondered. "Geez, who would notice if I took money from such accounts?"

Brian started contemplating ideas for getting the money. He could pick a set of dormant accounts with a lot of money, reduce their balances, and put the total into a dummy account he made up. The program code wouldn't take more than a day to write and run. So long as the total of the amounts he reduced equaled the money he put in his dummy account, the affected bank ledger would balance, causing no alarm. The next day he could do electronic payments to pay off the $75,300, then delete the dummy account to cover his tracks.

Brian put his plan into action the next week. By Friday he was debt free.

———

What led to Mr. Pierce's happy visit with Donna was her task as an auditor to find spikes in the dormant account report, to note unusual changes in account balances. "Boring as watching paint peel," Donna would occasionally lament. Spikes never occurred.

One day however, the paint peeled before her eyes. Eight account balances had changed from the prior week. They were reduced in total by $75,300.

Curious, she ran a query on all active customer accounts with balance changes of plus or minus $75,300 in the last two weeks. That might identify someone in the bank skimming dollars by stealing from dormant accounts.

Donna's eyes opened wide. Wednesday prior, one customer account had a new balance of exactly $75,300. She went online to see what the current balance was. The account was no longer on the system. No customer name could be traced.

Whistleblower time. The situation was bigger than Donna. It required a team of investigators. She notified her boss to take it from there. His eyes opened wide too as he grasped the details and reached for the phone.

Within a week the fraud perpetrator was found, and Mr. Pierce was notified of Donna's key role.

———

"Brian, where are you, honey?" Donna was on her phone inside the entrance of Frost's restaurant. The mirror behind the bar reflected her silky black evening dress bought specially for their engagement party that night. "We're here waiting."

Their friends were abuzz with rumors of a bank person getting escorted out the door that day by the police. Donna stopped short. Her fraud perpetrator?

That made sense given Mr. Pierce's morning visit. She kept quiet though. Her knowledge of the matter was confidential.

Still no Brian after an hour of cocktails and gossip.

Crestfallen, Donna gave in. "Everyone...let's call it a night. I'll text you later when I've found Brian."

The night passed without a word from Brian. Donna was on her couch in her apartment, sick with fear of not knowing his whereabouts. At 6 a.m. her phone rang. "Ramsey Adult Detention Center" appeared on its face.

She sat up. "Hello?"

"Donna?" It was Brian's voice – but from the county jail?

Perplexed, Donna said, "Brian, are you OK? What's going on?"

"I need you to post my bail."

Suddenly it came to Donna – Brian was the thief she had caught, the bank person under arrest.

Furious, she said, "You stole from the bank?"

Now it was Brian's turn to be confused. How could Donna know that? "I can't say right now,

Donna, but I need your help getting me out of here so I can clear things up."

Donna's reflex was to hang up on Brian. She did.

—

Saturday and Sunday crept by with no call from Brian. Donna stayed in, sleepless and forlorn, fraught with unknowns. Monday at the bank was hell. Staff stared as she wound her way to her desk. She imagined her new title – fiancé of the bank embezzler. Other than two trips to the women's restroom, she stayed hunkered down in her cubicle all day which left her spent and starving by day's end. Then she got the call.

"Hello," she said. A whisper was all she could muster.

"Donna, I am so sorry."

"What the hell, Brian?" Anger took over.

"Donna, I'm in trouble…"

She interrupted. "Can you please explain to me how you got arrested on the day of our engagement?"

Brian did his best, but Donna's young heart went stone cold as he spilled the truth of his gambling and deceit. It was too much to take.

"Brian, I need time to think."

Dead silence.

"Brian?"

"Donna, I'm still in jail."

"Well…I don't see how I can help. You stole from the bank. I unknowingly caught you. How can you expect me to help you now? I'm sorry, Brian. I can't."

Their last words fell into the abyss of a dying relationship and the call ended.

—

Brian spent two weeks behind bars. Bail was finally posted by his parents, rather his whole family as none in his clan had much equity to put up.

While in jail, he and Donna had two more phone calls. She listened to his promises to right things, but his depressed state and weak persuasions painted a dismal picture.

A future that included waiting out Brian's prison time and coping with his addictions felt too grim for Donna. Insurmountable. And she being the rumor mill's main subject at work had become unbearable. It all added up to misery Donna was not willing to endure. She decided to start her life over – leave Brian and quit ONE Bank. She gave notice to both the week Brian was sprung free.

Brian took the news hard. Their last call was brief, with Donna standing firm.

"Donna, you've abandoned me," were Brian's last words.

"This isn't about me supporting you," Donna replied. "You've brought this on yourself. Ruined both our lives. I'm sorry Brian, I have to move on."

On her last day at ONE Bank, Mr. Pierce again graced her narrow cubicle opening.

"Donna, here is my personal letter of recommendation. Please use me as a job reference. I'm sorry to see you go."

She stood. "Thank you, sir, I will." Mr. Pierce left with a nod and a polite smile.

Donna sat down and swiveled in her chair for the last time. She stopped on the third spin, then took a deep breath and rose up toward her new life.

• • •

Yellow

Wilerd, Texas

2019

Naomi looked pensively down the 5K running path on the grounds of Bjorke Consulting. There she had maintained her fit and smoothly curved thirty-four-year-old body since her start at Bjorke seven years ago. Normally her happy place, Naomi's expression that Friday reflected concern. Not from her job or the steep incline ahead. She'd mastered both long ago. Her anxious look had to do with the coming Monday – eloping with her fiancé Derek.

The source of her anxiety centered on a secret Naomi had been harboring since her teens. One that could eventually erode the underpinnings of her marriage with Derek, like slow rust eating away a sound bridge.

Her need, her true want since thirteen was to share her life, her body, her soul with a woman not a man.

Affluent Wilerd County Texas, where she'd lived her whole life, was no place to be gay. She would've been cast out of the circles she traveled, and her family's reputation trashed by the county's gossip jackals.

That fear had kept Naomi on the straight and narrow in the past, dating men for the image of being "normal". Fun was certainly had. She was no wall flower. But boredom usually ended things in six or seven months. She channeled the between stretches of loneliness into advancing in her career at Bjorke, which at least made for financial success.

With Derek things were different. The last three years had been a lasting distraction from her other want. The whirlwind of his devotion and love, his softer side and witty humor, the fun of his seemingly endless wealth, and the glamour of being next to him in Wilerd high society were joyful. He loved their physical intimacy. The time had arrived naturally for marriage and a family.

Life looked and felt good on the outside. But, inside Naomi felt a void, like she was marrying her best friend. Something was missing in it all.

As she started down the 5K path, the clock to Monday felt like it was spinning faster than ever.

—

Typical for a Friday happy hour, Frost's Pub on Division Street was packed with professionals downing a bump or two before heading home. Reprieve from their long week in the glass towers of downtown Wilerd.

Naomi stopped in for a stiff scotch to sort out what to do about her pending life with Derek.

She worked her way to the only open spot at the bar. The pub's brick wall was on the left and an interesting looking woman sat to the right.

"Is this seat taken?"

"Nope, all yours," said the woman. She followed with a pleasant smile.

Naomi lifted her right leg high and swiveled on to the barstool. A tricky maneuver in her skirt. Its length revealed a desirable figure but nothing beyond. A move like that in one of her skimpy designer dresses would have been a different story and not even attempted.

Naomi's 5K derrière did not go unnoticed by the men tabled north of the bar. Same for the woman next to her.

Naomi settled in. "Thanks, I'm Naomi."

"Nice to meet you. I'm Carri."

Naomi caught the bartender's eye. He was at the wash station moving highball glasses up and down on a fixed brush in a foamy sink. "What can I get for you?"

"Dewar's, neat please," said Naomi.

"Me too, Mathew." Carri's glass had half to go. She looked back at Naomi. "No gaps allowed in Friday night scotch drinking."

Naomi returned a knowing smile. "Good plan."

Carri's attire was loose, cool, and urban. It draped a body that knew physical activity. A riot of colored specs rode white cotton cloth from her shoulders down and onto her baggy olive pants. Acrylic paint from flying brushes, Naomi guessed.

"So, you paint?" Naomi asked.

Carri leaned a bit into Naomi's space and tilted her head, clearing strands of blonde hair from her eyes. Green eyes that sought Naomi's brown ones. "I do," she said.

Naomi liked the subtle intrusion of Carri's nearest forearm. A few missed streaks of yellow paint flattened the fair peach fuzz on her skin.

"You have yellow in progress?"

Carri looked down and laughed. "Good eye. A big abstract I'm doing told me it needed yellow. I'm not sure I agree, but a painting knows better than me where it's headed, so I usually listen."

The drinks arrived. "Both on me," Naomi said to Mathew as she went for her first sip. She let the liquor's warmth linger on her tongue, anticipating the mental relief to come.

Carri was beyond that, full-on feeling good and wanting more conversation.

She got her wish. To start they touched on life's matters, then delved into Naomi's passion for art and Carri's creation of it.

"I would love to see your work, your studio sometime."

Carri pointed toward the pub exit sign. "Three blocks on foot and we're there."

Two more scotch with a shared shrimp cocktail, followed by a three-block walk to the Wilerd warehouse district got them to the freight elevator of the renovated building that housed Carri's art studio condo.

Arriving on the eighth floor, Carri led Naomi by the hand through dim hallways to a double-wide steel door lit by a bare bulb hanging on two twisted wires.

Naomi felt aroused by Carri's strong hand yet tender hold.

"Home sweet home," Carri said as she drew her key and unbolted the beast of a door. With a push they crossed the threshold into a huge space of open wood floor, surrounded by exposed beams and raw brick 14-foot walls. City light flooded in softly, defused by rectangles of hazy glass panes that made up the entire street-facing wall.

Carri flipped on the lights, walked to the room's center and gave Naomi a guided tour in place by pointing and rotating. "Kitchen, bed, bathroom through that door, yellow painting, me."

The yellow painting stood next to her on an easel seven feet high. Two shades of yellow fell purposely across a New-York-minute of white space. Dark neutral gray played anchor in the center.

"I absolutely love it. The painting, It's balance. It's impact. Wonderful." Naomi's eyes left the painting and returned to Carri. "So, how long have you been here?"

"Going on four years now." Carri pointed at another dozen canvases leaning on the wall, surfaces as big as the door they just came through. "These are works in progress too. All demanding my disciplined un-discipline, if that makes sense. The first big sale of my life got me enough down payment to buy this place. I've averaged six sales a year since then. Starving artist, no more."

"You followed your passion. Its hardship. I love that. I see it in the yellow one."

This response felt real to Carri – Naomi got it. Carri took an unplanned next step.

"Well...I've gotta get out of these painting clothes. Why I wore them to the bar is beyond me. In a rush for scotch I guess."

Naomi had been in the same frame of mind earlier on her way to Frost's. "God, yes." She eyed two bottles of wine hugging the corner of the kitchen island. "Should I pour us something?"

"The Pino please. If you like. Glasses are above the toaster." Carri grabbed fresh clothes from a wall shelf and disappeared into the bathroom.

Naomi snooped in the kitchen. Counters, sink, and floor spotless. Fridge half-stocked of healthy makings for one person. Ben and Jerry's hard in the freezer. Pictures and cards on the fridge door all smiles. Their magnets traveling the typical souvenir/fix-it path. Niagara Falls. George's Plumbing. Chester Toyota. Flag of Texas. Betty Boop.

She chose two wine glasses with long delicate stems and poured a generous amount of the Pino in each. As she sat down on the couch the bathroom light clicked off. Carri came out wearing a low cut, thin cotton T-shirt and fleece sweatpants. She tossed her paint clothes on the floor by the laundry basket. When she turned toward the couch the wall of city light made a brief silhouette of her small breasts and erect nipples.

She walked over, plopped down opposite Naomi, and reached for her wine in a prolonged fashion. Her hands smelled of lavender. She allowed the V-neck opening of her shirt to completely reveal what was silhouette ten feet ago. In response, Naomi touched the back of Carri's hand to keep her breasts in view longer. Their eyes met and held.

The mutual seduction in play cooled to safe conversation for a time.

A lull in talk arrived. Both women sat silent. Their postures spoke instead. Naomi's right hand toyed gently with Carri's left. They had leaned closer while sharing confidences and stayed there.

Thinking of Carri's body, and her obvious interest in hers, Naomi felt an urgency, an attraction to Carri she'd not known with a man.

"Oh my God," she thought. "This feels so right. Everything about this feels right. This is what I've always wanted."

Breaking the moment, Naomi said, "Carri, this is going to sound crazy, but I have to go."

Carri leaned back. "What...did I do something wrong?"

"No. No. It's not you at all. It's me. It's just that I have to fix something in my life before this can happen."

"But I thought..."

"Carri, I'm sorry...I just need a chance to get my head together. Can I have your number? Call you after I get things straightened out?"

"OK by me."

Contact info swapped, Carri walked Naomi to the door. They put their arms around each other and pressed close for a long minute, said goodbye, and Naomi was gone.

—

From his voice alone, Naomi could feel Derek's mix of disbelief and rage. She should've waited until morning.

"You can't marry me? Naomi...Naomi, what? Why for God's sake?"

"I do love you. I do…but…"

"But, what? We're getting married in two days. You're calling it off?"

"I have feelings that are making it hard."

"That makes no sense. I thought we were happy together."

"Feelings...about being with another woman."

Derek paused.

"A woman? What woman?"

"Not a particular woman...but...someday maybe..." Naomi's voice trailed off. This was impossible.

"You're lesbian? Now all of the sudden? What in the world did we have for the last three years? You were just pretending to love me?" Derek's words twisted out of his throat with a painful harshness.

Naomi froze, not knowing how to proceed. Coming out. Breaking Derek's heart in the process. She cared for him. And there she was wrenching his future away, a future rich with possibility. One they had co-conceived.

"Say something." He was flat angry now.

"Derek, honey...can I see you? Talk to you face-to-face about this?"

Before Derek had a chance to reply, Naomi's phone sounded a call-waiting ringtone. The caller ID said "Carri Bingham". In a panic, Naomi accidentally put Derek on hold and took Carri's call.

"Shit. Shit. Shit," came flying out of Naomi's mouth.

Shocked, Carri hung up.

When Naomi got back to Derek, his line was dead.

—

Naomi shifted the bouquet of flowers and knocked on the double-wide steel door.

All was silent.

She knocked again.

Silence. No one home.

She placed the flowers in the doorway, so their yellow petals caught the best light from the lone bulb above. Message said, she silently slipped away.

• • •

Remy

St. Anthony Village, Minnesota

1969

"I haven't seen my dick in twenty years," Stosh shouted.

That sent chuckles through the other two old-timers perched that afternoon in the four-chair waiting room of Springer's Auto Repair, where they met daily for ten-cent vending machine coffee and local talk.

"What you get, having a beer belly da size of a keg."

The volley came from Stosh's left. He turned to his accuser. "You watch it there, Stanley. Your belly gets in the room three minutes before you do."

Stanley looked down. There was a good chance he hadn't seen his dick for decades either.

Earl, the last of the three amigos as they were called, took advantage of the lull. "Can we change the subject, please? How about Killebrew's homer last night?" It was 1969 and Minnesota Twins' Harmon Killebrew was having a worthy season of home runs. The topic was a sure bet to switch the gears of conversation.

Remy laughed at the guys' chatter coming through the waiting room door that led to his shop bay. Stosh's hearing aid batteries were low again causing his companions to carry on in shouts to avoid the need to repeat themselves, inadvertently allowing Remy to overhear them above the din of auto repair.

Remy was the ace mechanic at Springer's. Customers loved him for his honest estimates and quality work. When he rolled a car off the hoist it was fixed. His other claim to fame was stock car racing. He walked on water in the eyes of the three amigos in that sport. He was a young racer, sinewy strong with sharp reflexes, crafty on the racetrack, outwitting all drivers except Mad Bruce who was sponsored by Sid's Gas, the rival station kitty-corner across the street.

Mad Bruce was tied in points with Remy out at Raceway Park, the local quarter-mile oval track on the outskirts of the village. The last race of the season was one day away. It would determine which race driver would be the summer's champion and which shop could put the winner's trophy in the front window for all customers to see. The three-foot-tall trophy, all shiny silver and lit from above, drew people and their business in and provided gloating material during the long winter months when the track was closed.

Mad Bruce got his nickname from driving like a madman in his hellbent determination to cross the finish line first. He was a braggart and dominated all conversations. His race car was riddled with dents from the intimidating smacks he used to force past other drivers.

Remy on the other hand was known simply as a good guy. Soft-spoken, nice to talk with, but just as determined to get to the finish line first. His car had its dents too, but they came with apologies later if he was at fault. His preference was to slip by other drivers as graceful as possible, leaving them frowning in his dust.

Remy was finishing up an oil change for Stosh. He was on the last step, checking the air pressure in the four tires and spare. When he opened the trunk he hollered, "Stosh, what are these chains doing in here?" They were heavy-duty with hefty hooks at each end. It took work to get to the spare tire and top it off with air.

Stosh got up and strode into the shop. He was spry at seventy-nine, still capable of doing the work of a man half his age, although only for an hour or two. "Them's logging chains from the old days. I keep 'em in there for traction. You ready for Mad Bruce tomorrow night? Gonna be a big crowd."

"Ready as ever," Remy said as he resituated the chains and gently closed the trunk. "All done, Stosh."

The men stepped outside to survey Remy's car. Mad Bruce's car sat across the street at Sid's. Hand-painted black numbers on the doors of each identified the drivers for the spectators in the stands. Remy was "19" and Mad Bruce "03".

The cars were on display to attract attention, each car body exhibiting the scars of the season. Some of the "03" body paint showed on "19" and vice versa.

Orange on red and red on orange. Evidence of the rivals' dueling to get ahead in a race.

"Dat Mad Bruce, he is a cheater. Look at all them dents," Stosh observed.

"Well," said Remy, "I have a surprise for him tomorrow night. A new factory four-barrel carb. More power than I've had all summer."

"Dats good. Real good, Remy. You just make sure you keep the rubber side down. You'll win."

It was time for Stosh to go visit his mother, so he made a move toward his car and the men retreated from the hot sun.

"Put the work on my tab, Remy," Stosh said as he slid into the driver's seat.

"Will do, Stosh. See you tomorrow night."

Stosh gave a wave and took off. Oil change euphoria struck – a car lover's perception that all was well in the world with fresh oil and lube. He pictured a smooth cruise to Raceway Park with the amigos, then rubbing shoulders with them as they downed cold beer with stock cars flying by at death-defying speeds fifty feet away. He rode that thought until he pulled into the stubby driveway of his mother's house.

Lenka had pork chops, dumplings, and sauerkraut waiting when her son opened the door. The savory aroma got Stosh's taste buds lit up right away. Lenka was ninety-eight and still on her own with a mind sharp as a tack. She "did just fine, thank you" using her walker to get around. The house was orderly and spotless as always. Her food that night was a familiar comfort and her neighborhood gossip witty. Stosh stayed for the nine o'clock news, then kissed Lenka good night and left for home, sure that his mother was in good shape until his next visit a few days later.

Everything in the village was closed and dark when Stosh passed through. Corner street poles cast their light in patches here and there. It was under one such light that Stosh caught a glimpse of someone next to Remy's race car out front of Springer's. He took a hard left in front of the place to get a closer look and saw the silhouette of Mad Bruce fade into the shadows of the alley on the south side of the shop.

Stosh pounded the steering wheel. "What the devil is dat son of biscuit up to?" With the chance for any confrontation gone, he went home and had a restless night of Mad Bruce circling his quarter-mile dreams.

Stosh was on the shop driveway standing by "19" when Remy pulled in the next morning.

"Remy look at this," he hollered. Remy walked over, puzzled at Stosh's crack-of-dawn presence. Stosh pointed. A very slight amount of something white rested in the cove of the race car's gas cap. "I saw Mad Bruce here last night in the dark fucking with your car."

Remy touched the substance to his tongue. It was what he suspected. "Sugar," he said. "Mad Bruce put sugar in my tank. Oldest trick in the book."

The sugar-laden gas was a surefire way to shut down the car if it got into Remy's new four-barrel carb.

"Dat fucker," Stosh said.

"Stosh," Remy said coolly, "you saved the day. I'll take it from here." He left for his shop bay and prepared to roll "19" in for a gas tank flush that would reverse Mad Bruce's evil deed.

Stosh however was not so cool. He exited the shop driveway, looked left to Sid's place, and thought, "Dat Mad Bruce. He needs a lesson." He gave "03" a hard glance and instantly had the solution.

—

Race Night

"Stosh, why on earth are you lugging a chain around in that gunny sack?" Earl posed the question as the three amigos walked the pit area of Raceway Park on their way to see Remy.

They were on an arc of dirt road cut into the forest just south of the track. Off to the side, drivers crouched over and under their cars putting on final touches for the race heats to come. Sweat soaked tee-shirts stuck to their bodies from the muggy August night air. Stosh's polyester shirt was drenched as well from carrying the weight of the chain.

"Dat chain's for me to know and you to find out," said Stosh.

"Tryin' to lose weight to see your dick?"

Stosh gave Stanley a half-smile but had no time for a retort. They had reached Remy's pit area. He was cleaning the windshield, the last detail before strapping himself into the cockpit for the first heat.

The men started talking shop – how the car was running, what the tire setup was, and what Remy's strategy was to beat Mad Bruce. At one point, Remy winked at Stosh and said, "No sugar tonight in my coffee." Stosh laughed and nodded, then left the conversation. He stood on his toes looking for Mad Bruce and found him down the row shooting off his big mouth with some press reporters. His pit area was two over from Remy's and "03" was sitting unattended, front end facing out ready to go.

Stosh saw his chance of putting his get-even plan into play. He slipped away unnoticed and snuck into Mad Bruce's pit area. On his hands and knees, he unbagged the logging chain then hooked one end of it to the metal strap holding up the "03" gas tank and the other around the base of a tree nearby. The rusty chain lay with some slack and blended into the dirt in the dim light. You'd have to be looking hard to see the hazard Stosh had set. He stood up, brushed himself off, and started casually back, almost bumping into Mad Bruce right in front of Remy and the amigos.

Mad Bruce paused. "Howdy boys. Nice night to eat my dust, eh?"

Stosh stood aside and replied, "Good luck with dat, dickhead. Keep an eye on your fuel."

Mad Bruce gave Stosh a scowl, then walked on puzzled by the reference to fuel. Given last night's tampering, he was counting on Remy's car dying after a few laps from bad fuel, not his. No time to worry. The first heat was starting shortly, and he had to get to the starting line.

The three amigos hustled their old bodies out of the pit area as all the race cars started up. The noise was deafening and the air noxious with spent fuel. They got to their spot in stands as the first car entered the track.

When it came time for Mad Bruce to merge into the stream of cars headed for the track, he noticed a bump from the rear as he eased out of his pit area. "Just a stump," he figured and gave more gas. The place was dotted with low lying stumps easy to catch in the soft dirt. The powerful motor pulled "03" away no problem.

Remy and Mad Bruce pulled up to the starting line even, followed by fifteen other racers all raring to go. Remy gave Mad Bruce a wave and got a sneer with a middle finger back in return. "Geez he is a dickhead," Remy thought, then focused on Flag Man Bud up in the flag stand waiting with the green flag to start the heat. At once, Bud leaped in the air waving the green flag in figure eights and the racers were off and running. Remy and Mad Bruce got out front immediately and led the pack.

Stosh could not account for Mad Bruce making it to the starting line. The logging chain surely should have pulled the gas tank off the "03" chassis. And Mad Bruce had no time beforehand to spot the setup and unhook things.

The answer came in lap four when the rear end of Mad Bruce's car blew up in an orange ball of flame. Instead of laying back in the pit area, the gas tank had been dragging and sparking the whole race. He was down on the inside lane with Remy on his right. The explosion took control and forced his car straight across the approaching turn. Remy fought his steering wheel but had nowhere to go but straight off the track too.

The stands went wild. The three amigos stood as tall as possible but could only see smoke rising from behind the gap in the guard rail. Stosh collapsed back on the bleacher. His chest was tight. He needed air.

—

Three ambulances were called to Raceway Park that night from Village Medical Central. Mad Bruce ended up in the VMC burn unit. Stosh landed in intensive care for his heart. And Remy was taken directly to the VMC morgue. He didn't make it.

—

Death defying became death realized for the village in the last race of 1969. In the months that followed the three amigos turned to two waiting for Stosh to get out of jail. Remy's shop bay fell into disrepair. And Bruce never raced again.

• • •

POEMS

Green Beans for Maija

Tonight, Maija had green beans

For the first time

A small thing in one's life

To have green beans

For the first time

A tiny milestone

But one worth noting

For someday Maija will ask

When did I have green beans

For the first time?

And her mom will say

Your Aunt Sara

Braved wintery roads

For your green beans

For the first time

Second Language

Teaching English to birds is hard without a whiteboard.

My Dad's Hammer

I drop my dad's hammer on my garage shop floor.

I hear the ping as its steel head meets hard cement.

A memory is triggered of roast beef aroma floating

Well done through the garage window.

Supper nearly ready. Mom's roast beef.

Red potatoes. Something green. And orange Jell-O.

A drop of sweat leaves the tip of my dad's nose

And splashes down on a blue chalk line

That his saw removes in a smooth stroke.

Ten hours of hand tools on plywood

And the new shed is half done in the August heat.

I lob a 5' 4" hook shot from the front lawn

As he makes a grab for his hammer and misses.

Ball. Net. Swish.

Hammer. Cement. Ping.

The Space Between

What resides between my ears?

I can't sense anything sloshing around

In the space between.

I doubt there is anything really there.

But let's say for a moment there is something there.

Like my brain, as some would say.

If so, I find it ironic that it can sense

So many things except itself.

I still doubt there is anything between my ears.

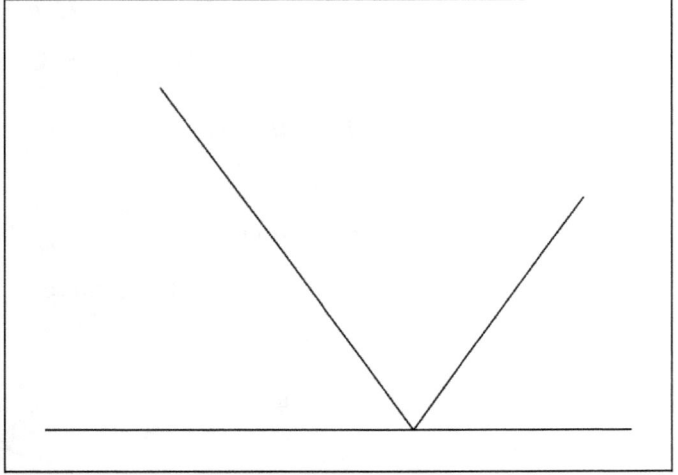

Brake Time

When a ray of light

Bounces off a mirror

It comes to a complete stop

Before it reverses direction

As it takes pause

From its speed of light

Does it wonder

Why

Thoughts Go

Where do thoughts go? For example, this paragraph. It resides here. And shortly it will reside in your mind for you to ponder. I wonder how many thoughts I have pondered in my entire lifetime. And how many of those I will convey to others. Which makes me realize that the collection of my thoughts are two things – the set that I originated, plus the set that others have conveyed to me. I wonder what my collection of thoughts weighs. Some thoughts defy gravity. Some sink me. A pound of feathers versus a pound of lead. I guess when I die the thoughts in my mind are gone forever. However, those I've conveyed to you will carry on. That is where thoughts go.

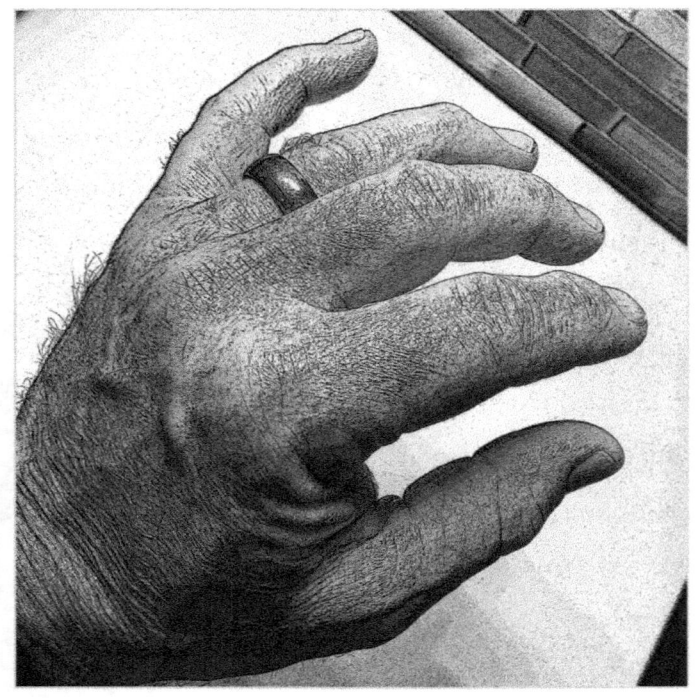

My Left Hand

My left hand. Always in the shadow of my right hand.

My right hand is my go-to hand. Gets all the glory,

While my left hand does the servile tasks.

Holds what is being dealt with on the right.

Smiles while my right hand presses the flesh.

Shows the world my marriage to Theresa.

Assists in what my right hand gets me into.

It is the asdf of things.

It longs to hit enter.

want

Heavy Letters

Profound sentences weigh more than shallow ones.

The letters that make up the words in

Profound sentences are physically heavier

Than the letters in shallow sentences.

That is the source of profundity.

Heavy letters.

Start

It is important to start what you finish.

DAVID RALPH JOHNSON

A LONG STORY

DAVID RALPH JOHNSON

Path of a Bullet

And the Innocents Along the Way

Chapter 1 – New Porch

Minnesota

July 1955

The drop of sweat finally left the tip of carpenter Steve's nose. It had been rocking there gently for a minute gathering courage for free fall. Courage found, the sweat released and splashed squarely on the head of Steve's next nail. The nail was unmoved. Not for long. Bang. Bang. Bang. Steve's hammer brought the nail home, through one board and into the board below. The nail's shank married the two boards together into a porch railing.

"Man, it's hot," Steve said to no one. He had the shadeless job site to himself. His other carpenter buddies had moved on to the next story-and-a-half house coming to be in newly sold off potato fields north of Minneapolis. Post-war treeless suburbs were spreading like spilled milk into the farmlands around the city in 1955, providing Steve and those in his trade with steady money.

Steve reached into the nail pocket of this tool bag and found two lone nails hiding out. The rest of the pocket was empty. Finishing the porch railing called for three nails. "What the frig?" whispered Steve. More nails meant a long walk to his truck down Penn Avenue, which was little more than a clay-mud-boot-sucking trail than a suburban street. Grading and pavement were a month away.

"Well forget that noise," he said. "Shortcut time. How 'bout I put one nail at the end as normal and the other in the middle. That'll hold." Once painted no one would know the difference. He secured the rail end with the first nail, then eyeballed the midpoint and drove in the second.

Steve glanced up. "There you go, baby," he said to the house. "Last nail for you. A little bit off, but it'll do." Steve's final hammer stroke completed the railing and the construction of the house. The next pounding noise would be happy kids' feet running around inside their new place. Steve smiled at that thought as he gathered up his tools and started toward his truck. Someday his two toddlers would have such happy feet. Two years, maybe. God willing.

Chapter 2 – Lead Ore

Utah

July 2015

Jerome brushed galena ore dust off his boots as he sat on the long bench in the Eureka Mine crew room. Bulbs in cages threw grim light on locker doors stickered with American patriotism and union devotion. Jerome's day job with fellow miners was freeing galena ore from Utah earth with properly placed TNT and not getting blown sky high in the process. If a blast didn't kill him, ingesting the ore dust off the job would do it, although that took a decade or two. The ore was laden with lead, a sure killer when accumulated in the bloodstream. Avoiding that called for thorough cleanup at the end of his shift every day.

After the ore's extraction and smelting, its lead would end up as bullets on the business end of cartridges made by OT Ammo a few states away in Rosebud Missouri. Lead for bullets started with Jerome's hands on TNT. Hands he now scrubbed hard so he could hold his guitar cleanly and hopefully his girlfriend Rachel later that night after his stint at Eureka's Whole Note Tavern.

""Scuse me Jerome." A miner named Lefty inched by. He brushed Jerome with his bad right arm. Miners shared tight spaces all day long.

"You sure smell pretty," Jerome said in a falsetto voice. Smelling pretty was an unusual thing for Lefty. "What you got lined up tonight?"

"Broasted chicken," said Lefty, avoiding the real reason for his fragrance.

"Smellin' pretty for a cooked chicken. Well you'll have to fill me in on how that turns out."

"OK, I'm seein' a girl kinda steady. Her name is Jane. She's cookin' me a meal tonight."

"Yup, that's worth smellin' good for," said Jerome. He got a backhanded wave from Lefty at the crew room door as he headed for daylight and Jane's chicken.

Jerome switched gears. With Rachel in mind, he hustled his cleanup, punched out on the time clock, and got to his pickup just as locomotive 4014 was revving up in the Eureka railyard, getting ready to run a week's worth of ore to the lead smelter in Rosebud.

The 4014 was hitched to a long string of gondola railcars. Black smoke poured from its diesels. Five hundred tons of stationary ore were introduced to three thousand horsepower and after a pregnant pause, the ore started creeping down the track.

Jerome's pending exit passed squarely over the rail tracks. He had a hundred yards to cover to beat the 4014. If the locomotive cut him off, it meant a prolonged wait as the train crawled out of the railyard. This was a weekly event – an event train engineer R.Tingle dreaded for the possibility of t-boning "that moron Jerome"; but one Jerome enjoyed as a thrill to kickstart the night to come.

Jerome smiled and gunned his engine. R.Tingle steeled himself and kept his stubby hand down on the throttle.

"I hope I let the moron have it tonight," R.Tingle thought. "Take out the back half of the pickup's box and stop this stupid game. Not kill him though. Just disable him for a month or two."

The race commenced and Jerome's pickup covered his distance with a second to spare. R.Tingle caught the flash of Jerome's grin as he bounced over the rail tracks, crossing just in front of the 4014's cowcatcher. "Nuts. Missed the twerp again," R.Tingle lamented, but inwardly glad for no catastrophe.

The 4014's line of black smoke crossed harmlessly with the red dust plume trailing Jerome, making a perfect X from above that marked the spot of their next contest.

Jerome got to the Whole Note on time, but Rachel was nowhere to be found. She arrived later though with her red dress on. That noticeably upped the passion in Jerome's one-man show. R.Tingle and his crew would reach Rosebud as scheduled with the full load of galena ore ready for smelting.

Chapter 3 – Four Shorts

Missouri

August 2015

"Come on Billy. We're gonna miss the Eureka train if you don't hurry." Tommy was already on his bike as he called from the backyard, trying to get his brother moving.

"Tommy, you leave Billy be. He's got toast crust to finish." The boys' mom June required clean breakfast plates before their morning adventures could begin.

Billy washed down the final crust with the last of his chocolate milk. He was good at eating food so things ended dead even. All evidence of breakfast gone, June pulled the trigger on the morning starting gun with, "You boys be careful on those bikes. And stay away from the tracks." Billy flew out the door and threw a "We will ma" back over his shoulder as he made a beeline for his bike. "Lord keep them safe," June said to little Jesus above the sink.

The boys headed out on a dirt path the width of their bike tires. Their destination that morning was the Rosebud smelting plant to see the arrival of the half-mile long ore train from Eureka. Houses on the end of Rosebud where they lived were spread out over dusty terrain. The closer you got to the smelting plant, the sparser the settlements. Noise and stinking air were the deciding factors on proximity choices out there. With mostly uninterrupted areas to roam, kids on their bikes had worn dirt paths over the years directly to and from points of kid interest. Highlights were the smelting plant railyard, a spring filled abandoned quarry, the cliff above the county dump, and the airport beacon tower. One kid, Handsome, had a moped to gas power himself to those places. All other kids depended on good breakfasts and strong skinny legs for their locomotion.

The bluff above the smelting plant railyard offered the best view of the goings-on. Handsome was there when the boys pedaled up. They got out a "Hey

Handsome" with their last breaths. The bluff was quite a climb. "Hey Harts," he said, "clear as a bell out here today." Smog from the smelter was blowing the other way for a change.

"Did ya git it?" Tommy asked.

"Yup." Handsome reached into his backpack and produced a horn that looked the shape of their bike horns. But it was longer, with a can of seriously compressed air for its base. The three boys had pooled their money three weeks ago for a means to communicate with the train. Handsome had procured a handheld boat horn from God knows where. It was certainly up to the task. They sought loud and Handsome found ear piercing. Goats three miles down the Rosebud valley were about to wonder when the Queen Mary would arrive.

"Excellent," said Tommy. He mastered the spelling of the word last year in third grade and decided to give it a try now in public.

"What is it, Tommy?" said Billy.

Handsome hit the horn button. Question answered, everybody had to wait a minute to get their hearing back.

"Shit, that'll do the trick." Handsome used swear words sparingly, which the boys liked. Too much of a good thing always wrecked the good thing.

Off in the distance, they heard the train horn. Two shorts, one long, one short. That put it at the County Road OO crossing. Soon the locomotive's triangle of headlights would be visible as it entered the valley for the straightaway to the plant railyard.

"OK boys, four shorts when we can see the engineer." In the back of Handsome's Big Book of Trains, there was a chart of train horn signals that he had studied to be ready for this happening. "That means signal back."

"Wowee," said Billy. He ran a small circle with his arms out like an airplane.

"Geez, what's with him?" Handsome's forehead wrinkled.

Tommy shrugged but lucked out not having to attempt to explain his goofy (unkind people said dim-witted) younger brother's actions. Train lights had come into view and it was time. He loved his brother. Plane or train.

The boys aligned, with Handsome in the middle, near the bluff's edge. The train was moving at a pretty good clip. Engineer R.Tingle had his head out the locomotive's window taking on the cool valley air.

The moment having arrived, Handsome let go the four shorts and the boys held their breaths.

R.Tingle's ears perked up at hearing the foreign but familiar signal. He looked east and saw the boys on the bluff grinning back. "Now there's a rag-tag outfit," he said to his brakeman Sven riding shotgun in the cab. Sven looked over R.Tingle's shoulder. "Yah sure. Dem boys dey got da horn alright." They shared a laugh.

R.Tingle gave the boys two shorts back, acknowledging their signal. Then against train regs, one extra-long one.

"Whoop Tee Doo," said Billy. He circled the airport one more time.

Handsome and Tommy did windmill waves, but they went unseen. R.Tingle and Sven were back on the job, eyes on the approaching the railyard, tons of galena ore from Eureka to deliver.

"Thanks, Handsome," said Tommy. "That was the best ever." When you're four feet tall, beckoning a half-mile long train and having it respond was on the level of dragon slaying.

'Yah, that was so cool." Handsome stood a little taller in the boys' eyes. And in his own mind too. He bagged the boat horn for next week's ore train visit and turned for his moped.

"See ya."

Dragon slayed, the brothers parted for home, stomachs craving baloney mustard sandwiches, pickle chips, and two cookies if they finished their meals without a fight.

R.Tingle and Sven spent the noon hour dumping the ore, railcar by railcar, into giant hoppers to await the lead smelting process.

A relief crew showed up to deadhead the train back to Eureka. Shift over, R.Tingle and Sven grabbed bunks in the caboose and slept the return trip away, rocking and rolling in dreamland.

Chapter 4 – Hell's Kitchen

OT Ammo was out of lead for bullets. Demand had exceeded supply for the last three months. Gun season in the mountains and midwest was approaching. Droves of hunters had boxes of ammo flying out the doors of sporting goods stores all over. Times were good. Dads were bringing their sons along this year. Great for the ammo business, but that left Harold Johnson of OT Ammo scrambling for lead stock.

"Katy, what's the story? You promised me last week I'd have the lead today." Harold stubbed out his cigarette. The ashtray on his desk had a berm of grey ashes around it. Harold was meticulous about cleaning his desktop once a year just before the OT Ammo Christmas party. That was six months ago.

Katy was the sole customer support at Rosebud Smelter.

"Mr. Johnson." She felt the need to go formal given Harold was putting the heat on. "Smelter four at Rosebud broke down last week which caused the delay. Your lead will be on the road to you end of day tomorrow."

"That gets it here Friday." If there had been a man on the other end of the line Harold would have added "Jesus H. Christ." But Katy was a girl, so he left that off. "OK, sweetie. Tell your boss Burt he will be hearing from me if ten pallets of Eureka lead are not sitting on my loading dock this Friday." Pallets were heavy oak platforms on which lead ingots were stacked and secured for shipment. Ten pallets held a lot of lead.

"OK, Mr. Johnson. Have a good day." Katy clicked off before she could hear Harold's reply. He was creepy. The shorter the conversation the better.

"Hey Burt, that was old fart Johnson from OT. Is his lead going out tomorrow?"

Katy and Burt worked opposite each other in the business office at Rosebud Smelter, a cramped affair two stories up from the smelting plant floor. Their desks were next to a great window overlooking the entire smelting operation. It was bulletproof to fend off an industrial calamity or labor union uprising. Outside the window, cauldrons the size of school buses traveled by with bright orange molten ore sloshing around. Suspended on heavy chain, the fifty-ton beasts were directed by hardhat smelters who nudged inch long dashboard levers to get the ore to the plant's hellfire blast furnace. Its two-thousand-degree heat separated out waste material, resulting in 99.9% pure lead ingots on the output side of the plant.

"Yes," Burt replied. "It's almost ready to go. He'll see his ten pallets on Friday. Ah...coffee time sweetie?" He followed that with a midlife crisis wink.

"Geez, I gotta get a different job," thought Katy.

Chapter 5 – Ingots to Bullets

Ten pallets of Eureka lead sat soaking wet on the OT Ammo loading dock Friday morning. The pallets were transported from the Rosebud Smelter the night before, on an open flatbed semi under a star choked sky. Rain had started and the loading dock overhang was doing no good keeping them dry. Wind from the north saw to that. The lead ingots stacked and bound squarely on the pallets weren't affected. They were 99.9% pure. Quite indestructible.

Harold Johnson saw the lead that morning as his car bumper touched the executive parking sign that held his name. "Finally," he thought. "Now we can catch up on ammo backorders."

Most of the lead on the dock would be cast into the usual bullets for cartridges sold to customers of OT Ammo. The rest of the lead was destined for a special project Harold had going – a new bullet that was less resistant to air, lighter than normal, and more lethal to its target. It would fly farther and splinter on impact, shredding the flesh it entered. These were attributes sure to get the attention of customers and make money for OT Ammo. Harold would see that enough lead was set aside to get the new bullet on the shelves of sporting goods stores for sale that coming fall.

He left his car and started up the loading dock stairs. It was slow going. He was still recovering from accidently shooting the tip of his big right toe while testing ammo last month.

He caught Lloyd Dugan out the corner of his eye. Lloyd was on foot from the corner bus stop. He had paused his skinny frame to look at the load of lead.

Lloyd was top machinist at OT Ammo and had an interest in the goods. "Mornin' boss. Looks like I can get my molds online now. That the lead?"

"Yes sir. Fresh from Eureka. Molds ready?"

"Yup." Lloyd had machined a dozen molds perfectly to a very specific shape for the new bullet. He was skeptical about the big promises OT Ammo marketing people were making about a lighter bullet with greater range, but he kept his mouth shut. He got paid for making exact molds. It was not his place to question the higher ups. That practice kept him on the job for thirty-three years and got his mortgage paid off in the process. Retirement was looking sweet for him and wife Marsha.

Harold smiled at Lloyd's response. He trusted Lloyd. Tens of thousands of OT Ammo bullets had flown true thanks to his expert mold making. They went inside together, happy to be out of the rain and onto the new venture.

A week later seven grams of Eureka lead were cast as the first bullet of the new special design. It rode atop a polished brass cartridge case, fresh off the assembly line. Harold and Lloyd were there for the sendoff. "Bullet One," Lloyd said as he picked it up and gave it an approving look over. He passed it to Harold who rolled it back and forth in his palm and smiled. It felt sleek like it really could fly forever. "Make us some money, sweetheart," he said as he put it back on the conveyor belt.

Ritual over, Harold said, "Nice work Lloyd. Again."

"Thanks, boss."

Lloyd hit the green GO button. The conveyor belt started with a lurch, then carried Bullet One smoothly away to be packaged with its comrades that were following right behind. Boxes labeled *New Design Special Aerodynamics Greater Range* were ready and waiting.

Chapter 6 – On Display

Minnesota

September 2015

Donna ran her hand across the tape that sealed the box. No way she could open the box barehanded.

"Geezus, OT Ammo knows how to get a box to North Minneapolis without it falling apart. Elvis, honey, borrow me your box cutter for a minute, please."

Her ask was directed at "Elvis" Presley Franklin. Presley slipped the box cutter from his belt loop and handed it off to her.

"I'm on break," he said. "Back in fifteen. Don't lose my knife." His words bore slight disgust. Donna pissed him off pretty much daily, always asking him for help. Her pay was fifteen cents more an hour and he was the one that really kept the Howling Wolf Guns stockroom running right. That burned him.

"You're in a good mood today," she replied, pouring gas on the Elvis flame. He stomped off.

Donna slit the tape on the top of the box, splitting the seal. The box flaps flipped open exposing a dozen smaller boxes full of OT Ammo cartridges.

"Well, lookie here. A new kind of bullet from OT. 'Special Aerodynamics Greater Range.' My, my, ain't that impressive?"

Shiny brass showed from tiny cellophane windows in the ammo boxes. Donna unlocked the back panel of the gun display case and placed the new ammo boxes in two neat rows. Bullet One stood at attention in its box, front and center, ready for action.

Chapter 7 – Purchase

IN GOD WE TRUST. ALL OTHERS PAY CASH.

April looked at the sign above her head as she ran a brick through the front of the gun display case in the quick in-and-out move of a practiced thief.

"Payment by brick tonight," she thought.

Shattered glass fell into the case and onto April's tennis shoes. She reached through the havoc and grabbed a box of OT Ammo and a handgun to match. She figured she had three minutes to get out of the Howling Wolf Guns shop before law enforcement came screaming up the hill. Plenty of time to exit the front door and melt into the teenage crowd forming in front of Tiny's Cellar across the way.

"The sooner the better," her bladder urged. She really had to pee, having spent three hours hiding scrunched down in the middle of the gun shop's coat carousel. There she had waited for the shop to close, giving her the opportunity to rob the place once Donna and lame-brain Elvis had vacated the premises. She knew them from high school, but they traveled in different circles. Donna and her two friends were snobs. Elvis ran with geeks. He tried to date April once. No way. April was a loner, with one exception – her relatively recent friend Kiara.

A few months back, new to the neighborhood, Kiara walked up to April at the morning bus stop and said, "Hey girl, where do you get a boy 'round here?" In short time, April could not go long without Kiara's unwavering optimism. And Kiara found April a quiet mystery with stories to tell – of which gun theft was now a new chapter.

April stowed the ammo and gun in her coat pockets as the Howling Wolf Guns silent alarm howled through the phone line to AACE Security down on West Broadway. Second shift Albert looked up from his Psychology II book and saw the 10-62 code on the bank of AACE alarm monitors. Break-in at the Howling Wolf Guns shop. Or a false alarm like last week when a squirrel bit through a wire in the same vicinity. Adrenaline kicked in, switching Albert's brain from an anxiety disorder characterized by irrational fear on page 103 to a frantic search for the phone. Phone found, he speed-dialed the police. Sargent Harris picked up. "North Precinct Minneapolis, Sargent Harris here. May I help you?"

"Yes, Sargent. This is Albert at AACE Security. I have a 10-62 in progress at the Howling Wolf Guns shop."

"On it," Sarge replied. He hung up and left to get his boys rolling. Two squad cars hit the street a blink later, lights screaming but sirens silent. Better to sneak in than warn a burglar of their approach.

As North Precinct's finest pulled up to the scene, April had already slipped through Tiny's crowd and found relief for her bladder, secure with her new gun in a graffiti peppered stall, out of sight from authority. The responding officers found the gun shop door locked with no sign of forced entry. April's exit from the inside out left the door closed and locked behind her. The coat carousel blocked the smashed case, covering her tracks.

The officers piled back in their squad cars, did a U-turn that many in Tiny's crowd noted as illegal, and headed for donuts and black coffee. Later, Sargent Harris posted "squirels agin" on that night's activity report.

Chapter 8 – Repair

Abel slipped his hammer from the loop of his tool belt. His sister Ida's house was a wreck. She bought the house cheap a few months ago with inheritance money from a favorite relative's recent passing. The gift allowed her to pay cash and avoid a monthly mortgage payment. A fortunate windfall for Ida and her daughter Kiara. Ida faced a lot of work to get it livable. Abel came over on weekends to help. They were lucky to have him.

It was hotter than blazes that afternoon on Penn Avenue, unusual for September in North Minneapolis. Abel decided to tackle just one outside job for the day – the loose porch railing. Sixty years of people and winters had taken its toll. The head of a nail stuck up in the middle of the handrail, just enough to catch skin or cloth. It would be an easy fix.

Abel looked at the nail. "Huh," he said to no one, "Somebody slacked on this work. Shoud'da used two nails." He hammered the nail back in place, leaving a slight dimple and chipped paint. "Putty 'n fresh paint, then good as new." He left for the garage as niece Kiara and her friend April ran up the stairs. No nail caught Kiara's hand this time. "Good work, Papa." She loved her uncle, the most dad she had known in all her thirteen years. Abel loved her right back for the happiness she brought him and Ida. She was a good steady kid in spite of life's odds stacked against her.

The girls went into the house and directly to Kiara's bedroom. Kiara grabbed the top journal from a stack of five and they returned to the porch, crashing onto its ocean of a couch. The couch was where Kiara wrote every day, where she parted from adolescence and poverty on a magic carpet of imagination. She rode her words to exotic lands and kind people. April traveled along now too, drawn in as their friendship had grown.

The porch's high ceiling provided shade and a mild breeze was cooling, a reprieve from the heat Abel was working in. "Hey Papa, you OK out there?" she asked as he returned from the garage.

In his youth, when he burned with energy, Abel would have been sweltering. But now heat felt good on his joints, even with bib overalls covering most of his three hundred pounds. "Won't be long here. Got curtains to hang inside for your momma. Hi April."

"Hi, Mr. Abel." April replied with some hesitance. She liked the old man but was still working up courage to trust him. Men in April's life were abusive, worse since she was maturing.

"Be sure to have a drink of water, please," Kiara said.

"I will, sweetie. What you girls writin' about today?"

"We're lost in a desert but have a sturdy camel and a handsome guide."

Abel smiled. "How many tents?"

Kiara caught on. "Three of course."

The all chuckled. April loved the quick wit of the household.

"OK, I've had it out here. Have fun writin'." He skipped the last of the work. The sun shone directly on the railing, too hot for putty and paint. "I'm headin' in."

"'K, Papa," Kiara said. She and April returned to the desert. The camel needed water. And Abel left to hang the curtains for Ida.

As suppertime neared, April rose and stretched. "OK, gotta go. See you tomorrow at the bus."

Kiara closed the journal, ending their word adventure for the day. "'K," she said, then after a pause said, "Thanks April."

"For what?"

"For being my friend."

Kiara's words filled a long-empty hollow in April's heart. Without pause, April wrapped her arms around Kiara. She could think of nothing to say to match the rush of joy she felt. Words didn't matter. Her hug did the talking.

After a moment, they parted, smiling and knowing tomorrow would be another day to share together as best friends do.

With the supper over and dishes done, Abel gathered his stuff and said, "Delicious as usual, Ida. Goodnight girls." He got his big body moving and out the door he went toward home. Ida plopped down in the living room to crochet and Kiara returned to the porch to resume writing. The heat of the day had subsided from Penn Avenue. Neighbors she didn't know yet walked by in the cool evening air. Kiara slipped a quilt over herself to keep the chill away. Its checkerboard pattern took on the shape of a girl on the verge of becoming a young woman. She drifted off to sleep around her bedtime, laying in the comfort of the quilt, and dreamt of swimming with the handsome desert guide, now her true love, in a blue oasis pool.

Chapter 9 – Boxing

Next block over, at April's house, Dick downed the last of the vodka. The cat clock above the back door read 2:15. Or 1:15. It was hard to tell. The clock hands were a blur. The cat's eyes and tail swung back and forth oblivious to the time. No help there. His wife Angie was way overdue regardless. Out again with friend Dorothy drinking his hard-earned wages.

As the clock hands moved to 2:16 or 1:16, the backdoor knob twisted slowly. It was Angie attempting a quiet entry to not disturb Dick who was hopefully out cold on the living room couch, his place of sleep the last six months.

Dick, being quite awake, fired off a "Where the hell have you been?" from his corner of the kitchen. A boxing ring without the ropes started to materialize. Startled, Angie slammed the back door shut. Family dog Stealth figured it was a good time to go and evaporated.

"Jesus Christ almighty Dick, you scared the hell out of me."

Angie took her corner of the ring and slipped her gloves on.

April was down the hall in her bedroom waiting for round one to begin. Fight night again. Sporadic in her youth, now it was a hellish routine event.

Her mom threw the next verbal punch. "Dick you're drunk. Go to bed."

April's stepdad countered with a long sentence that included "slut" and foul profanity. He then crossed the kitchen ring and punched her mom in the face. There was no alcohol on Angie's breath. She rarely had a taste of the stuff. The taste on her tongue now was blood from a split lip.

April felt the cold smooth curve of the trigger. The gun she stole yesterday rested loaded, lethal, and heavy in her right hand. Bullet One was third in the gun clip, ready for flight. She clicked the safety off.

Angie swung back at Dick. Her two small fists landed left and right on Dick's chest, doing no damage.

Furious, Dick grabbed her wrists and threw her to the floor.

Stomped down. Defeated. Angie pleaded in a soft voice. "Stop, please stop, Dick."

April trembled with rage hearing those words. It wasn't the first time. Now though, she held the means to end Dick for good. End the insanity of him. She flew from her bedroom, down the hall to shoot Dick dead.

Seeing her mom on her hands and knees sobbing, she stopped short of the kitchen, readied herself, and proceeded in with the gun in both hands like she'd seen on TV. A string of bloody saliva dripped in slow motion from her mom's mouth as April closed her eyes and pulled the trigger three times.

The first bullet went into Dick's liver, the second his heart. The third bullet, Bullet One, went high and out the backdoor as the gun barrel rose in April's hands. It wasn't needed. Dick was ended.

DAVID RALPH JOHNSON

Chapter 10 – Oasis

Bullet One pierced easily through the single pane of glass in April's backdoor. It flew free now with the late-night air it's only impediment. It was designed for this. Sleeker. Faster. Farther. It passed in the split of a second over the backyard and between two houses, then crossed Penn Avenue with Kiara's house dead ahead.

From the ocean couch, Kiara dreamt on of the desert guide she and April had contrived. She ached to hear him say her name. But he was silent. She would be patient. Dreams cannot be willed.

Bullet One entered Kiara's yard at an angle. It sped silent, faster than the sound it made, and skimmed the porch railing, colliding with the nail Abel had righted the afternoon before, the nail that carpenter Steve had hammered home sixty years ago where it shouldn't have been.

In her dream, Kiara's eyes met those of her guide. Their glance held the point of no return. The point of surrender. When two become one, unencumbered in a faraway land.

The nail's head sent Bullet One ricocheting slightly off course, through the porch screen door and into Kiara's chest, shredding her heart and stopping there.

A strange comfortable warmth enveloped Kiara and her guide as they embraced. Everlasting love found; Kiara's life was complete.

• • •

THE LENGTH OF NOW

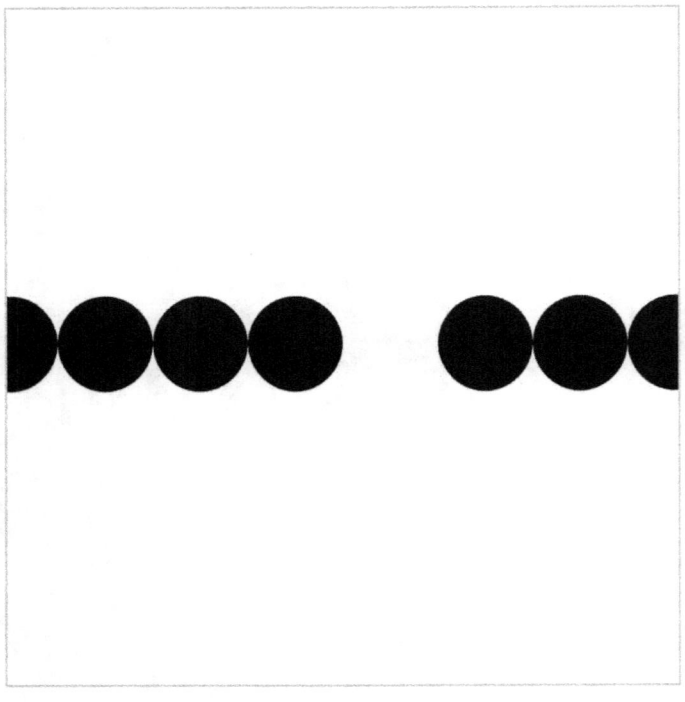

The Length of Now

You are only in the moment for an instant.

Epilogue

Casting the net took place over the last three years. What I salvaged is reflected in the assortment of stories and poems you have just read. That's it for The Length of Now. More soon.

David Ralph Johnson

ABOUT THE AUTHOR

David Ralph Johnson is a writer and photographer. He lives in Menahga Minnesota with his wife Theresa, and memories of their old dog Jake.

www.ingramcontent.com/pod-product-compliance
Lightning Source LLC
Chambersburg PA
CBHW070326120726
47909CB00008B/2619